1. Ella's First C

Ella was excited but ı first day of gymnastics class. She had always watched her friends perform flips and cartwheels, but the idea of doing it herself felt impossible. Her coach told her to take it one step at a time. Ella practiced, falling a few times, but each time she got back up and tried again. Her coach reminded her that every gymnast starts somewhere, and every mistake was just a step toward improvement. After weeks of practice, Ella finally did her first perfect cartwheel. She realized that courage is about trying even when you're scared.

2. Maya and the Vault

Maya had always dreamed of flipping over the vault, but she was terrified to try. One day, her coach asked her to focus on the feeling of soaring through the air. Maya hesitated at first but decided to give it a shot. She took a deep breath and ran at full speed. As she vaulted into the air, her heart raced, but she landed perfectly. Maya was filled with pride. She realized that the key to success wasn't avoiding fear but facing it with determination. Every time she conquered her doubts, she became stronger.

3. Lila's Big Beam Challenge

Lila had always struggled with the balance beam. The narrow surface seemed impossible to conquer, and she was afraid of falling. Her coach encouraged her to focus on the center of the beam and trust her body. At first, Lila wobbled, but with each attempt, she improved. Then, during an important practice, she managed to stay on the beam for a full routine. Lila beamed with pride. She learned that balance wasn't just about physical strength; it was about mental focus and believing in yourself.

4. Rosie's Resilience

Rosie had a natural talent for gymnastics, but when she faced a tough fall, she doubted herself. She wasn't sure if she was cut out for this sport anymore. Her coach sat with her and explained that every gymnast faces setbacks, but true success is about how you get back up. Rosie decided to keep going, even when things didn't seem easy. Her resilience paid off when she mastered a difficult move she had been struggling with for weeks. Rosie learned that perseverance is key—sometimes, the greatest success comes from the hardest struggles.

5. Grace's Determination

Grace had always been the underdog in gymnastics. She wasn't the fastest or the most flexible, but she had a heart full of determination. As the day of her regional competition approached, Grace worked tirelessly on her routine, practicing every movement until it felt like second nature. On competition day, she was nervous, but she reminded herself that she had done her best in preparation. Grace performed her routine flawlessly and felt an overwhelming sense of pride. She knew that effort and heart were just as important as talent.

6. Mia's Perfect Split

Mia was known for her flexibility, but she dreamed of doing the perfect split. It seemed impossible, and she felt discouraged when her muscles resisted. Instead of giving up, Mia started to stretch every day, listening to her body and being patient with the process. One day, after weeks of practice, Mia finally achieved the split she had been working toward. Her coach smiled and reminded her that flexibility is built through consistency and patience. Mia learned that nothing worth achieving happens overnight —it's about steady effort over time.

7. Lily's Leap of Confidence

Lily had always been a little shy, but gymnastics gave her a chance to step out of her comfort zone. She struggled with her beam routine, but each time she practiced, she gained more confidence in herself. During an important showcase, Lily stepped onto the beam and performed her routine with poise and grace. She realized that the real victory wasn't in her performance—it was in how she learned to trust herself. Lily understood that confidence isn't something you're born with; it's something you build through belief and practice.

8. Zoe's Supportive Team

Zoe loved gymnastics, but sometimes she felt like she wasn't as strong as her teammates. They could do flips and vaults she could only dream of. One day, during a team practice, Zoe made a mistake, but instead of feeling embarrassed, her teammates cheered her on. They reminded her that gymnastics wasn't about competing with each other; it was about lifting each other up. Zoe felt a surge of gratitude for her team. She realized that the greatest strength in gymnastics comes from the support of others, not just individual achievement.

9. Ava's Dream Routine

Ava had always looked up to elite gymnasts and dreamed of performing a perfect routine. But it felt like a far-off dream. Every day, she practiced hard, focusing on improving little by little. She wasn't always the best in her class, but she worked diligently. One day, after months of practice, Ava performed her dream routine at a talent show and nailed every move. She realized that with enough dedication, dreams can become reality. Ava learned that consistent practice is the bridge between where you are and where you want to be.

10. Emma's First Back Handspring

Emma was scared to try a back handspring. It seemed impossible and dangerous. But her coach told her that the key was trust— trust in herself, in her coach, and in the process. Emma practiced slowly, using a spotter, until she felt confident. Finally, one day, she did her first back handspring without help. She was overjoyed and proud of herself. Emma realized that when you trust the process and stay determined, you can achieve things that once seemed out of reach.

11. Olivia's Vault Victory

Olivia had always struggled with the vault. The thought of running at full speed and jumping over the bar felt daunting. Her coach encouraged her to break the process down into smaller steps, working on her run, jump, and landing one at a time. Olivia practiced tirelessly, overcoming each challenge. Finally, she was able to clear the vault and land a perfect dismount. She learned that breaking down big challenges into smaller pieces makes even the hardest tasks achievable.

12. Lily and the Perfect Cartwheel

Lily had always been afraid of doing a cartwheel, convinced she would fall. But she was determined to overcome her fear. Her coach reminded her that falling is part of learning. With time, Lily's body began to understand the motion, and soon, she was doing cartwheels across the gym. Lily learned that success isn't about never falling—it's about getting back up and trying again with even more determination.

13. Mia's Flexibility Journey

Mia was amazed by how flexible some of her teammates were. She wanted to achieve the same level of flexibility but wasn't sure how. Her coach showed her how to stretch properly and consistently. Mia worked on her flexibility every day, gradually increasing her range of motion. Over time, her flexibility improved, and she felt stronger and more confident in her movements. Mia learned that flexibility is built through patience, consistency, and dedication.

14. Zoe's Gymnastics Story

Zoe had always been the quiet one in class, but gymnastics gave her a voice. As she improved, she became more confident in her abilities. One day, she landed a perfect routine and felt proud of how far she had come. Zoe realized that gymnastics wasn't just about physical skill; it was about self-expression. She understood that gymnastics helped her find her inner strength and confidence.

15. Ava's Never-Give-Up Attitude

Ava was determined to master her back handspring, but she fell many times and felt like giving up. Her coach encouraged her to keep going, reminding her that gymnasts never give up—they just keep practicing until they succeed. Ava finally mastered the skill and realized that her determination was more important than the number of times she fell. She learned that success isn't measured by how many times you fall but by how many times you get back up.

16. Rosie's Routine Challenge

Rosie had always been a perfectionist, which made it hard for her to accept mistakes. One day, during a practice routine, she stumbled and missed a move. She was upset at first, but her coach told her that gymnastics is about progress, not perfection. Rosie took a deep breath and completed the routine, learning to embrace her mistakes as part of her growth. She realized that striving for perfection wasn't as important as learning and improving over time.

17. Grace's Teamwork Triumph

Grace's gymnastics team had been struggling to perform their group routine. They kept missing moves and losing synchronization. But instead of getting frustrated, they decided to work together and support one another. After practicing, they finally perfected the routine and felt like a true team. Grace realized that teamwork is essential in gymnastics. When you support each other, everyone shines.

18. Emma's Solo Success

Emma was nervous about doing a solo routine in front of the entire gym, but she decided to give it her best shot. She practiced every day, fine-tuning every detail. On the big day, Emma stepped onto the floor and performed her routine flawlessly. She realized that performing solo helped her grow in confidence, showing her that she was capable of doing things she never thought possible.

19. Mia's Leap of Faith

Mia had always been afraid of trying new things, but gymnastics taught her to take risks. When it came time to try a backflip, she was terrified. But her coach believed in her and encouraged her to trust her abilities. Mia took a leap of faith, and with the support of her coach, she landed the flip perfectly. Mia learned that sometimes, the biggest victories come when you step outside your comfort zone.

20. Zoe's Champion Spirit

Zoe had always wanted to be the best gymnast in her class, but she quickly learned that being a champion wasn't about winning medals. It was about pushing yourself, staying focused, and supporting others along the way. Zoe worked hard every day, and when she achieved her goals, she realized that the journey itself was the true reward. She understood that being a champion is not just about winning—it's about growing and being the best version of yourself.

21. Lily's Leap of Courage

Lily had always wanted to do a backflip but was terrified. She practiced for weeks, building up her strength and confidence. On the day she decided to try, she took a deep breath, flipped, and landed perfectly on her feet. Her teammates cheered, and she felt a rush of pride. Lily learned that courage isn't about not being afraid; it's about trying even when you are. Each step forward makes you braver than before.

22. Zoe's Stronger Self

Zoe struggled with the uneven bars at first. She felt nervous every time she had to swing and release. But after months of practice, she finally found the rhythm and made it across without hesitation. Her coach told her that gymnasts are made stronger by their struggles. Zoe learned that challenges help you grow and that it's okay to take your time. Becoming stronger doesn't happen overnight—it's a process.

23. Ava's Dream Dismount

Ava had been practicing her dismount on the balance beam for months. Each time she tried, she felt unsure. But her coach reminded her that mastering a dismount took time and patience. Ava kept working, focusing on her landing. Finally, during practice, she stuck the landing perfectly. Ava realized that sometimes the hardest skills are the most rewarding to master. She learned that staying focused, no matter how hard something seems, can help you achieve anything.

24. Emma's Consistency Pays Off

Emma was always consistent in her gymnastics practice, but she never felt like she improved as quickly as her teammates. One day, her coach told her that the key to success wasn't talent—it was persistence. Emma continued to practice day after day, and soon she noticed that her skills had improved more than she realized. Emma learned that even when progress feels slow, consistency will always lead to improvement.

25. Maya's Patience

Maya had big dreams of competing at the state gymnastics meet, but her flexibility wasn't where she wanted it to be. Her coach explained that flexibility takes time and should never be rushed. Maya made stretching part of her daily routine, working slowly to improve. Months later, her flexibility was better than ever. Maya learned that patience and consistency were essential in achieving her goals.

26. Grace's First Floor Routine

Grace had been working on her floor routine for weeks, but something always felt off. She couldn't get the timing just right. Her coach worked with her on small adjustments, and after lots of practice, Grace finally performed her routine flawlessly. She learned that even when something doesn't feel right, every small change can make a big difference. Success comes when you keep trying and refining your skills.

27. Ella's Big Competition

Ella had always been nervous about competitions. When she finally reached her first big meet, she was scared of making mistakes in front of a crowd. But her coach told her that gymnastics is about performing for yourself, not others. Ella took a deep breath and went through her routine. Even though she didn't get everything perfect, she was proud of herself for staying calm and performing her best. She learned that success is about doing your best, not being perfect.

28. Rosie's Trust in Her Coach

Rosie was struggling with a challenging move on the bars. She didn't think she was capable of it, but her coach kept encouraging her. One day, after weeks of practice, Rosie finally executed the move perfectly. Her coach told her that trust and hard work were the keys to success. Rosie learned that believing in her coach and herself was the way to overcome any obstacle.

29. Zoe's Routine Reflection

Zoe was upset after a competition where her routine didn't go as planned. But when she watched a video of her performance, she saw that she had made huge improvements from her last competition. Zoe realized that success isn't always about winning; it's about progress. She learned that each time she performed, she was getting better, and that was worth celebrating.

30. Mia's Commitment to the Basics

Mia was frustrated with not being able to land her new skill. Her coach reminded her that even the best gymnasts spend time working on the basics. Mia spent extra time strengthening her basic skills—her jumps, kicks, and form. Slowly but surely, she saw improvement in her new skill. Mia learned that building a strong foundation is essential for tackling more difficult moves.

31. Lily's Positive Attitude

Lily always had a positive attitude, even when things didn't go as planned. One day, she fell during a practice, but instead of getting upset, she laughed and got back up. Her coach noticed her positive energy and praised her for it. Lily learned that a positive attitude can turn setbacks into opportunities for growth and improvement.

32. Ava's Supportive Friend

Ava's friend Zoe was struggling with a new routine, and instead of focusing on her own practice, Ava decided to help her friend. Together, they worked through Zoe's routine, supporting and encouraging each other. Ava learned that true friendship in gymnastics means helping each other grow. Together, they became stronger.

33. Rosie's Self-Belief

Rosie had always been self-critical and doubted her abilities. But during a practice, her coach asked her to perform a routine she had always struggled with. When she did, she was amazed at how well she did. Rosie realized that her self-doubt had been holding her back. From that moment on, she believed in herself more, knowing that she was capable of achieving great things.

34. Emma's Focus

Emma was easily distracted during practice, which made learning new skills difficult. Her coach taught her a technique to focus on one thing at a time. Emma began to concentrate on each move, focusing all her energy on it. With her new focus, she was able to perform better and learn faster. Emma learned that focus and concentration are essential to success in gymnastics.

35. Mia's Team Spirit

Mia was excited to compete, but during the competition, her teammate stumbled. Mia quickly offered a word of encouragement, and they both finished strong. Mia learned that gymnastics is about supporting each other, whether you're competing or practicing. Team spirit, she realized, is just as important as individual performance.

36. Zoe's Calm in the Storm

Zoe had always been nervous about performing under pressure, but during a big competition, she decided to try a new approach—staying calm and focusing on her breathing. With her nerves under control, she gave one of her best performances. Zoe learned that calmness under pressure can lead to amazing results.

37. Grace's Never-Ending Effort

Grace was working on a difficult routine that didn't come easily. She practiced every day, putting in the effort and never getting discouraged. Eventually, she performed the routine flawlessly. Grace learned that no matter how long it takes, consistent effort will always pay off in the end.

38. Ava's Overcoming Fear

Ava had a fear of heights, and the uneven bars seemed too high for her to handle. With the support of her coach, she faced her fear little by little, getting comfortable with the height. Slowly, she gained confidence and conquered her fear. Ava learned that facing your fears, no matter how big they seem, will always lead to growth.

39. Emma's Fearless Focus

Emma had always struggled with performing in front of others. But one day, her coach asked her to perform her routine in front of the class. Emma focused on the routine and blocked out everything else around her. When she finished, her coach was impressed with how well she performed under pressure. Emma learned that focusing on the task at hand can help you perform your best, no matter who's watching.

40. Lily's Perfect Timing

Lily struggled with her timing on the floor routine, but her coach reminded her that timing comes with practice. After working hard for weeks, Lily finally felt the rhythm and nailed her routine. She learned that practice, repetition, and patience can help you master even the most difficult skills.

Printed in Great Britain
by Amazon